Number Two

Dorling Kinderlsey
www.dk.com

Editor Fiona Munro
Designer Lisa Hollis

Published in Great Britain in 1997
by Dorling Kindersley Limited, 9 Henrietta St, London WC2E 8PS
This edition published in 2000

A CIP catalogue record for this book is available from the British Library.

ISBN 0-7513-6702-8

Color reproduction by DOT Gradations
Printed in Hong Kong by Wing King Tong

Number Two

COLIN AND JACQUI HAWKINS

Dorling Kindersley

"How do you do?"
said Number Two.

"I'm the fastest Numberlie in Numbertown."
Number Two lived in a blue house
with two yellow windows
and two red chimney-pots.
It was the second house in Numbertown.
The address was 2, Number Lane.

Number Two had two
of everything.
There were two
cosy chairs
and two beds.

One, two,
up we go!

Sometimes
Number Two
slept on the top
bunk, and
sometimes on
the bottom.

As Number Two was such a busy Numberlie her two telephones were always ringing.

Every day, Number Two bought two newspapers. She read them both twice in two minutes.

"I'm very hungry," said Number Two.
"I'll make my favourite breakfast."

With a frying pan in each hand,
she cooked two golden pancakes and
tossed them high into the air.
In less than two minutes,
she had gobbled them both up.
"I'm the fastest pancake-eater in
Numbertown!" said Number Two.

Number Two had a bright yellow bicycle.
It had two pedals, two wheels,
and two handlebars.

She cleaned and oiled it twice a day.
"My bicycle is the best and fastest bicycle
in Numbertown, and I'm the fastest
Numberlie on two wheels,"
said Number Two proudly.

Every day at two o'clock, Number Two
set off on a two mile ride.
The yellow bicycle whizzed down
two hills, over two bridges,
and around two bends.

"Whee!" she laughed.

"You can't catch me.
I'm the fastest Numberlie."

One day, as Number Two raced around
the second bend, she saw two
ducks chatting in the road.
"Out of the way!" she shouted.
The ducks scattered in fright.
"You road-hog!" they quacked crossly.
But Number Two
just laughed
and said,

"You can't catch me.
I'm the fastest Numberlie."

The next day, when the clock struck two,
Number Two raced off again.
This time, as she sped around the bend,
she saw two fat pigs trotting up the road.
"Mind out, pigs!" shouted Number Two
as she zoomed past.
"You road-hog!"
they squealed angrily.

"Hee! Hee!" giggled Number Two.

"You can't catch me.
I'm the fastest Numberlie."

The next day, Number Two pedalled even faster along the road. Suddenly, she saw two enormous cows in the way. "Out of the way, cows!" she shouted. But the cows just stared at her.

The yellow bicycle swerved, hit the kerb, and Number Two flew into the air. "She's a real high flier," said the cows.

Bump! Bump!

Number Two hit the ground with a crash.

Help was soon on the way and Number Two was rushed to hospital.

"You need patching up," said the doctor,
"but you can go home in two days."
"Hello," said a voice. It was Number One.
He had a present for Number Two.
"You're not so fast now!" he laughed.
"Yes, I am. I'm the fastest Numberlie on
two crutches," huffed Number Two.

Number Two was delighted with
Number One's present. It was just what
she needed – two bells for her bicycle.
Two days later, she raced off around
Numbertown, ringing them
both at the same time.

Tring!
Tring!

"You can't catch me.
I'm the fastest Numberlie . . .
and now I'm the noisiest as well!"

laughed Number Two.